CHEATING

CHEATING

*Maintaining Your Integrity
in a Dishonest World*

Barbara Mary Johnson

Augsburg ■ Minneapolis

CHEATING
Maintaining Your Integrity in a Dishonest World

Scripture quotations unless otherwise noted are from the Holy Bible: New International Version. Copyright 1978 by the New York International Bible Society. Used by permission of Zondervan Bible Publishers.

Game cards from *A Question of Scruples*, Milton Bradley, copyright © 1986, are reprinted on pages 25 and 26 by permission of Hasbro, Inc.

Excerpts from J. B. Priestly, *Angel Pavement*, (Chicago: University of Chicago Press, 1958), copyright © 1958 by V. S. Pritchett, on pages 32-34 are reprinted by permission of Sterling Lord Literistic, Inc.

Excerpts from Liu Binyan, *People or Monsters?*, ed. Perry Link (Bloomington, IN: Indiana University Press, 1983), on pages 80 and 81 are reprinted by permission.

Cover design: Judy Swanson

Library of Congress Cataloging-in-Publication Data

Johnson, Barbara Mary.
    Cheating : maintaining your integrity in a dishonest world / by
  Barbara Mary Johnson.
      p.   cm.
    Bibliography: p.
    ISBN 0-8066-2443-4
    1. Honesty.   2. Integrity.   I. Title.
  BJ1533.H7J64   1990
  179'.8—dc19   89-14962
                                                                        CIP

The paper used in this publication meets the minimum requirements of American National Standard for Information Sciences—Permanence of Paper for Printed Library Materials, ANSI Z329.48-1984.   ∞™

Manufactured in the U.S.A.   AF 9-2443

94   93   92   91   90   1   2   3   4   5   6   7   8   9   10

To Betty,
who loved going on my book tour

Contents

Introduction

Students were cheating to get into class. That was the newest campus scandal that caught my attention more than three years ago. Graduating seniors at my university needed certain required courses to graduate, and they found a way to get them.

Student registration workers took the coveted class tickets for these seniors, their friends, before regular registrants had a chance to register.

That's when I started my research, only to find that cheating was everywhere—in the government, corporate world, and personal relationships. Newspapers, magazines, and TV were (and still are) brimming over with tales of fraud, bribery, and dishonesty, plus press reports on scandals about themselves.

I was bombarded by headlines, such as these:

- Noted scientist accused of research misconduct
- Grade-selling allegations cancel 3 college classes
- Cheaters prosper, risk is small, say brazen students

- Bush sternly warns about defense fraud
- Chilling omen of Pentagon fraud probe
- Speakes relates how he made up Reagan quotes
- Defense investigation involves leaks of secret data to contractors
- Big prize contests rigged
- Real cost of fraud: jobs of average workers
- JPL computer penetrated by a hacker
- Dodger pitcher accused of cheating
- Character, not chemistry, must take the gold
- Religious broadcasters ethics panel probing Trinity network.

With that spurring me on, I began circulating questionnaires asking individuals to give me their stories, as victims or victimizers of dishonesty. Answers poured in.

High school and college students, prison inmates and ex-cons, housewives and corporate executives, professionals in engineering and medicine and law, told me their tales. They communicated through personal letters, long-distance phone calls, several one-on-one interviews, and a taped conversation from overseas. Many thanked me for the opportunity to unload; several cautioned me to contact them only at their business address. To preserve their anonymity, I changed names and locales.

Above all, I am grateful to my correspondents for their openness. Their stories probably transformed my passing concern about cheating into a lifelong interest. I hope readers will also continue a pursuit into questions of integrity and fairness, catching the various messages delivered to us in the media—especially in news accounts.

As a journalism instructor I understand that good news is not "news" to the reporter, editor, or even their audience. Bribery, fraud, swindling, and corruption are news precisely because they are not the way we want to be. Dishonesty goes against the American ideal. Reporting such scandals keeps the subject before us, and that is a start in the right direction. After the press points its finger at troublesome areas, the public may be more likely to take action.

People are beginning to speak out against cheating and are doing something about it. For example, my university's class schedule now includes a paragraph stating the school's policy on cheating so students know that it can lead to expulsion. The journalism department now insists that all its professors include this warning on their course outlines. Experience has shown that merely pointing out the serious nature of cheating keeps most students honest.

Moral dilemmas became the discussion subject of my church's adult education class. We struggled over solutions to them by leaning on God's loving care as we followed a gripping, 10-week public television program on ethics. And we're not alone in our desire to find answers. I see the public's interest in ethics and integrity increasing. Such outrage over dishonesty can bring back honesty and fairness into everyday life.

We can look at Scripture. " 'Love the Lord your God with all your heart and with all your soul and with all your mind.' This is the first and greatest commandment. And the second is like it: 'Love your neighbor as yourself' " (Matt. 22:37-39).

In exploring the dilemma of a cheating world, I make many references to our love for God, our neighbors, and ourselves. God's free grace, or forgiveness, available to us through Christ, gives us the foundation for living lives of integrity. We know we are loved, accepted, and forgiven. We in turn are empowered by God's Spirit to love, accept, and forgive others around us and ourselves.

Knowing how much God loves us through Christ does not free us from our struggles, however. We still must deal with all sorts of deceit and cheating—lying, swindling, fraud, bribes, and plagiarism. But God guides us through his Spirit, Word, and through prayer. God also works through helpful people and stays with us in difficult times so we can live our lives with integrity.

As you read the following chapters, I hope you will begin to look at daily occurrences with new insight. You will find solutions to problems in unique applications of your love for God, yourself, and your neighbor.

PART 1

Sounding the Alarm

1

Dishonesty Has Many Faces

*Do not conform any longer to the pattern of
this world but be transformed by
the renewing of your mind.*

Romans 12:2

Debra sat down on the kitchen stool, dealing out cards
into piles, flipping the top cards face-up. There were five
more minutes before the school bus arrived. One eye on
the clock, she began to build red-and-black sequences with
her top cards, revealing the ones underneath. Debra's mind
raced through her day's schedule of cookies to bake, dry
cleaning to pick up, and her daughter's ballet class at four.

After searching the pack in her hand for a needed red
10, Debra peeked at one of the face-down cards. Nope.
Maybe the other one would be the 10.

What harm is there in looking? She smiled to herself.
It certainly doesn't hurt anyone, she thought, and then
everything will fall into place.

Debra found the red 10 and unlocked the log-jam as
she put all the cards in their home piles. Having it come
out right was satisfying. As her daughter walked into the
kitchen, Debra finished the game neatly.

But what did she hope to gain? There was no solitaire
trophy for her to put on the mantel. She wasn't going to

brag about winning her little game to the other parents at ballet class, although they might have been sympathetic.

Charlotte, a Maryland resident, once kept track of 150 solitaire losses in a row. That's when she decided to take control by arranging the cards into a winning game.

"I don't know why cheating on myself destroyed my pleasure in solitaire," Charlotte said. "But I circumvented the only challenge in the game, the element of chance. After that I quit playing."

Plenty of folks like to make things come out right. I know I have done my share. Like other frustrated game players, I just want to win. Is there anything wrong with that?

Only Hurting Ourselves

Cheating at solitaire is just the beginning as we look into the question of integrity. There are many other challenges we overcome neatly by stacking the deck. Some of us regularly rearrange certain snags in our daily life. We're not hurting anyone else, we say.

One of our favorite hurdles to get around, instead of over, is our fitness program. Fifty pounds overweight, Betty arrived at her first aerobics class feeling self-conscious in her black leotards. Why didn't anyone else have cottage-cheese cellulite? The rest of the women were wearing bright colors over firm muscles, looking as though they didn't need the class. Betty was there on doctor's orders.

While jazz blared with an insistent beat, Betty drifted to the last row, avoiding eye contact with the instructor. "By hiding in back, I could slack off when I felt tired or out of breath without the instructor yelling at me," Betty explained. "Who am I hurting? This way I get through those 50 minutes of torture."

When it's time for pushups in my aerobics class, I do the same. I slow down, tie my shoelace, or get a drink of water—anything to avoid an exercise that I know is good for me.

There's always next time to do better, I think. This is equally true with diets. I cheat with that bowl of crispy chips and spicy dip tempting me tonight, resolving to cut out junk food tomorrow.

If I'm sabotaging my health program, I'm only hurting myself. Right? If anyone dares to check up, I can rationalize that it's no one else's business. But what message am I relaying to myself? I'm telling myself that I'm not worth the extra effort to abide by a few restrictions.

Just Helping My Family

What about bending rules to help someone else? Ever do a friend's homework? I have. What about doing reports for your kids? Does that count as cheating? What about fudging on your tax return?

JoAnn wants the best for her family. She and her husband are at the buying stage of life. With three school-age children, a dog, and a cat, the family has plenty of medical and dental obligations, plus piano lessons to pay for, soccer uniforms to buy, and veterinarian bills to pay. They spend everything they make, including JoAnn's part-time wages as a bookkeeper.

Every year at income tax time, JoAnn puts in extra effort studying new tax laws and checking records she has accumulated. The biggest windfall to lower their tax returns is her paid-in-cash salary. JoAnn doesn't pay any taxes on it because she doesn't report it. "I'm helping my family," she said, "every way I can. Besides, lots of other people do the same thing."

Employers who list workers as self-employed vendors don't have to pay for any benefits for them and don't withhold any taxes from them, either. Helen, a tax consultant in Arizona, said this is the biggest problem she encounters. "Last year a young couple, hired by a contractor to do accounting and maintenance work, were surprised to learn they owed $4,000 in taxes. They filed returns honestly, but realized their employer was exploiting them. For next year, I told them to have their boss list them as regular employees or find other jobs."

Sometimes, Helen said, her clients confess their tax evasions to her. "One guy building swimming pools hardly showed any profit. I asked him how he lived on that. He said, 'There's plenty coming in under the table.' "

Yet Helen said most of her customers bend over backward to be honest instead of bending the rules. These conscientious taxpayers must carry an extra burden from those who don't pay their share.

How long before everyone joins this trend in tax dodging? Some observers say most people are already at that point, seeing no harm in such creative bookkeeping.

Are the Christian values of honesty and fairness that many of us learned as children being cast aside? You may hear that the way to success is through intimidation, that good guys finish last, and that it's OK to put yourself first. You often see neighbors and prominent public figures get ahead by dishonest means. The world seems to say that anything goes.

As a child, you probably learned you should "tell" if you broke the living room lamp. Stealing anything was forbidden. You were taught to share your sandbox toys and your crayons. Your family and peers taught you these values both by words and by example. In Sunday school and church you learned that following God's plan meant being honest and treating other people fairly. You saw Christ's perfection as a model.

But there are other values and standards of the world that intrude. You may be affected by the values of your peers more than you realize. For instance, if some of your friends approve of tax cheating, you may find it difficult to tell them you think it's wrong.

Just Helping Yourself

But how much harm can there be in a little misdealing—from solitaire, to diets, to taxes? How do deceitful practices affect your family, your neighborhood? What are the prevailing standards in your community? Do you know the ethical codes of the various agencies and systems that control your life?

These are questions to ponder when looking at the larger issue of cheating and dishonesty. Problems of deceit can range from cheating in school and driving above the speed limit to high-level corporate dishonesty.

While most people still are trying to follow the Ten Commandments and teach their children right from wrong, some have made subtle changes in their outlook. Today both students and parents have new ideas about what it means to do well in school.

Since I started teaching at a state university early in the 80s, I've seen students cribbing on tests with cue cards hidden away in pockets, cuffs, and back pages of the exam book. I've learned about some new ways to cheat, such as writing answers on calculator covers or storing answers in the calculator's memory.

Test papers are swapped in the hallways. Some students sit-in for their unprepared friends and take their exams for them. Students send away for instructor-manual exams from unsuspecting textbook publishers. Instead of studying their textbooks, these enterprising pupils simply study the test itself.

Not all students accept this approach to complete their college work. One student admitted to me that he had copied from a classmate in another class. I said I was surprised that he would tell me this one week away from our own exams. Collin's brown eyes widened as he insisted that he was a Christian and had learned his lesson.

He said he had been stuck for a math formula that he could see on a neighbor's paper, so he copied it. After the test, he confessed the misdeed to his teacher.

"But the professor didn't want to hear about it or do anything." Collin shrugged to show his disbelief. "I felt terrible about it, and I'm sure I'll never do it again."

A Cheater's Climate

Other students do not have Christ's love to rely on and come to other conclusions. In a high school in Connecticut, Scott said that failing students copy answers to keep their parents off their backs about flunking out. "Some just don't do well on tests but feel they deserve a better grade," Scott said. "So they crib."

Once this climate is established in a classroom, Scott said, good students realize they must raise their grades to stay ahead. Despite Scott's high IQ and good grades, he often used a "cheat sheet" for his physics tests: "Mostly because everyone else did, too. Well, there were a few exceptions."

Who is getting hurt in such classroom deception? Those students Scott called the "few exceptions"? What about the students who say they want and need a good education? Aren't they losing out?

Potential employers, clients, and patients may be getting less than they deserve. If we think about the long-range effects of test answers written "off the cuff," we might look at that med school diploma on our doctor's wall a little differently.

We're concerned here with who is being hurt by the rule-benders. At first glance it seems to be no one, or at least no one but ourselves. Then the circle of deceit broadens to include neighbors, friends, and more. Why do we hurt our neighbors when we are supposed to love them?

Accidentally Hurting Others

Mavis, a sales rep in northern California, did a great deal of traveling by car, at top speed. There are many like her on the Los Angeles freeways where I drive. I know what it's like to be driving 60 mph in a 55 zone, with everyone else roaring past me.

Mavis was one of those. To avoid speeding tickets she bought a fuzz buster. This device alerts her when police are tracking down speeders in the area. When the buzzer goes off, Mavis slows down. She said the device is good for her because it helps her get where she needs to go in less time. Perfectly legal, it even has a money-back guarantee.

Last spring she was driving at her usual 80-mph rate on a rain-slicked freeway, with two more calls to make before heading home. Speeding around a bend in the freeway, she didn't see a lumbering schoolbus in time to swerve. Mavis plowed into the bus, but her seat belt kept her from any serious injuries. However, the crash threw several children to the front of the bus. One 6-year-old girl's arm was so badly mangled that doctors advised amputation.

Who can we blame for the accident—Mavis, the rain, the radar detector company, lawmakers who allow such devices, or drivers who create the demand? Isn't there a public consensus that says it's smart to exceed the speed limit? Everyone is doing it; only the wimps obey the law.

Is that true? Only the little people obey the rules these days? Big business, with its enormous multinational corporations, often seems to be above the law. Dishonest corporate decisions threaten us all.

About a decade ago a woman was driving a Ford Pinto that stalled in the merge lane on a Minnesota freeway. Her car was rear-ended and exploded into a fireball fatal to her. A 13-year-old passenger survived but needed skin from donors so doctors could build a new nose and ear for him. Yet this accident could have been avoided if the Ford Motor Company had heeded warnings from its own engineers.

Mark Dowie, an investigative report writing for *Mother Jones* magazine, uncovered early tests that showed that the Pinto's fuel system ruptured easily. Retooling the assembly to correct the problem was deemed too expensive in Ford's cost-benefit analysis. The corporate officials preferred to risk it. If there were lawsuits, the corporation was prepared to pay the going price of a human life, set by the National Highway Traffic Safety Administration at less than $300,000.

"There are a few of us here at Ford who are concerned about fire safety," an anonymous Ford engineer told Dowie. "They are mostly engineers who have to study a lot of accident reports and look at pictures of burned people. But we don't talk about it much. It isn't a popular subject."

In fact, Ford lobbied strongly against government safety standards that would have forced the company to correct the Pinto's fuel tank. Dowie charged that the company lied in its campaign to block such a safety measure.

With these examples, we've gone from the solitaire card player in her kitchen to the board room of a large corporation. Is there a connection? Can we escalate from card cheating to powerful corporate or even governmental decisions that deceive millions of people? Can we find the answers in our Christian faith?

Striving to be in control, whether it's a card game or an empire, is the same old "trying to be God" game that Adam and Eve invented. We can find answers to the problem of maintaining our integrity by looking at the estrangement with God that follows such mistakes. We end up at odds with God, our neighbors, and ourselves. Yet God's forgiveness can set us in the right direction again, and we are motivated to strive for fairness in all our dealings.

We need to consider who is getting hurt by our missteps. We can try to become good examples for our neighbors and help our communities become aware of higher values, especially the ones we have learned from the Bible. We should be incensed at the dishonesty that surrounds us.

One of my favorite bumper stickers says, "If you're not outraged, you're not paying attention." To do that we need to recognize the many faces of dishonesty.

Questions for Reflection or Discussion

1. What examples of cheating have you seen in your community? Do some of them seem fairly harmless (cheating on a diet or while playing cards)? Which ones concern you?

2. Why is it so tempting to cheat when money is involved? Do you think our society places so much emphasis on money that we're willing to compromise our values?

3. If you are a student or can talk to some students, find out how common cheating is and how the schools handle it. Do students think it's OK as long as they don't get caught?

2

Rule Bending Is Everywhere

> *I hear the human race is falling on its face,*
> *And hasn't very far to go.*
> —Rodgers & Hammerstein, *South Pacific*

We don't like to hear words such as *bribe, fraud,* or *plagiarism.* We become incensed if someone calls us a cheat or a liar. In most of our social circles, we are too polite to mention swindling. After all, the Ten Commandments made it clear, more than 3000 years ago, that we shouldn't lie or steal from our neighbor. We know right from wrong.

But these forms of dishonesty are parts of our lives. We are victims as well as victimizers. There is even a popular game called *Scruples* that provokes speculation among the players about their responses to such temptations. The game is equipped with 252 cards posing dilemmas such as: "The only available spot in the parking lot is reserved for the handicapped. You are in a hurry and won't be very long. Do you park there?" And: "As a lawyer, do you defend someone whom you know is guilty of a vicious rape?"

The situations described on the cards make players decide whether or not their fellow players would lie or cheat. Players are forced to take ethical stands. Values usually associated with religious training have become part of a game.

Developed by Canadian Henry Makow, *Scruples* instructs its players to guess whether their opponents will answer yes, no, or depends. The subject matter is too sensitive for some.

When my daughter and son-in-law play the game, he becomes quite disturbed when his scruples are questioned. Some of their friends even refuse to play because they don't want to expose their scruples as entertainment for the evening.

Skirting the Truth

One of the *Scruples* game cards reads: "Your child has missed the age deadline for kindergarten by two weeks. You feel the youngster is ready. Do you misrepresent your child's age?"

Who are you going to be hurting if you fudge a bit on the child's age? Yet lying has been defined as the denial of another person's right to the truth. You're cheating someone out of something. In the case of kindergarten registration, your own child may be the "someone" who is cheated.

At any rate, dishonesty multiplies the number of "someones," just as ripples spread out from a stone tossed into water. Theologian Rudolf Bultmann said there are no innocent bystanders when we lie. He contended that our lies extend beyond our immediate space, back into our past, and into the future.

Images of our ancestors can be distorted by our dishonesty. Grandchildren and great-grandchildren—babies not even born yet—may be affected. Our decision to lie alters the lives of friends of friends of friends.

A college student confessed in a letter to Dear Abby that she had concocted a story of herself as a victim of child-rape. This tale won her support and sympathy from her friends who suggested she seek counseling.

"Well, I went," explained the young woman who signed the letter as "Forever Lying," "and told my counselor the same story I had told my friends. So now I am lying to him, too. I tell the story about my 'rape' so well that I am beginning to believe it myself."

How many people, besides herself, will be taken in by her story? Will she go so far as to accuse an innocent person of the rape?

As a bystander, you can easily be drawn into someone else's deceit. For example, your boss may ask for a little favor, which might be something you consider unethical. What do you do?

Teaching a course for school administrators, Sarah had judged one member of her class as a failure. The student, a sometime TV actress, hadn't attended class most of the time for medical reasons and showed a lack of interest in her studies.

However, she had friends on the school board and in other influential posts. Sarah's supervisor pressured her to give the failing student a passing grade. Against her best instincts, Sarah agreed to change the final grade to "satisfactory."

Two years later, a school superintendent who knew Sarah telephoned her when he saw her name on his new employee's transcript. He had hired the young student partly on the basis of her grades. "She doesn't know anything," the superintendent said. "How could you give her 'satisfactory' in your course?"

"I was mortified," Sarah recalled, "I tried to explain but it was no use. I was so ashamed of what I had done."

The ripple effect was magnifying her one misstep into several problems. A school district is saddled with an untrained administrator. A superintendent is distrustful of certain school records. And a conscientious teacher became painfully aware of long-reaching consequences of one mistake.

Taking Someone Else's Words

When I began teaching mass communication, I didn't know that some of my students might buy term papers for my class instead of writing them. Audrey, a graduate student of journalism in her early 40s, told me one semester that she was offered $50 to write a term paper for a younger student. The student's offer was no secret, either.

Several friends of the 20-year-old student argued her case before Audrey. They talked about the long hours her job required, how close it was to the deadline for the paper, and that she needed to graduate that spring.

Audrey spent 30 minutes trying to explain to the group why she wouldn't compromise herself for $50, or any amount. "What good is a high grade on a project you know nothing about?" she asked them. What is a degree worth, from a school that ignores cheating? Was this fair to other students who wrote their own research papers?

But the young students saw nothing wrong with the proposition. It was a simple business transaction.

A student in Quebec made a better deal. He used someone else's A-plus paper—for free—and the original author was accused of selling it. Ella had given the paper to this acquaintance who was taking the course one semester after she had completed it.

"My paper's subject was 'Wages for Housework,' " Ella explained, "and he said he was writing about women in Sweden. He only wanted to see the size, scope, presentation, mathematical content, etc., of a well-graded paper. I would have felt cheap to refuse to lend him the paper."

She didn't know he would retype it and hand it in as his own. In fact, he followed it so exactly, the professor pointed out, that he even copied a spelling error. The prof didn't believe that Ella was an innocent victim. He threatened to expel her if such a thing happened again.

Buying Support

We need to be savvy and constantly alert to protect ourselves from various forms of deceit. Bribery, for example, is a sneaky aberration.

Young women in short skirts were handing out free cigarettes and cocktails to hundreds of journalists at a national convention I attended in Phoenix in 1985. The Tobacco Institute rented a booth to reach news people in this way.

As a member of the ethics committee, I had a front seat to the ensuing ruckus. Committee members debated whether reporters writing about lung cancer or drunk driving would be compromised by free smokes and a drink of bourbon.

The public's right to know might be in jeopardy, the committee decided. Even if the small-scale bribery had no effect, the principle was wrong. The Tobacco Institute was asked to dismantle its booth and take its freebies elsewhere. The committee had high standards.

But some people are quite open to bribery. Such was the case in a West Virginia coal-mining town recently investigated by federal agents. Most citizens of Kermit, population 705, were so accustomed to selling their vote for $5 or a drink of cheap whiskey that they were actually surprised when 75 officials were arrested for graft.

One man who landed in jail boasted that he controlled 500 votes. A villager noted that "nothing has been going on now that hasn't been going on forever."

When a prominent family member in Kermit was tried for drug dealing in 1985, she bragged about payoffs for the jury hearing her case. "In the hallway, you could see people waiting to get their money," she said. "They were standing in line."

Consumers Beware

Stories about influence buying and political corruption may seem remote from our daily lives. But as consumers we are targets of fraudulent deals every day. Most of us have felt the sting from purchasing items that were less than what we bargained for.

Warren said he bought a phonograph set when he was living in New York City that came with lists of precautions to avoid starting a fire: "Don't do this, don't do that, don't do almost anything lest it start a fire."

"Also, the radio needed an antenna," Warren said. "I haven't seen a radio that required an attached antenna since the 40s when I was a little kid."

Another apparent swindle involved a school alumni-directory offer, for which Joe sent $50. After four months of waiting for the directory, he said, "I will feel cheated even if it eventually arrives because some of the addresses and phone numbers will be out of date."

Stacy, a theater major, fell for a $125 picture-directory offer that included a chance to read for movie parts. "I thought this was my break," she said. "Scams like this should not be allowed to be in business."

Scams can go both ways, sometimes preying on the vendor. A California landlady worked a scheme to get painters to decorate her property at little cost. After the first painter she hired completed three-fourths of the job, he was told to stop. The woman pointed out mistakes and shoddy workmanship. She fired the painter and refused to pay him. The scheming landlady quickly hired another painter to complete the job—one-fourth of the work at one-fourth of the full price. Longtime tenants said they had seen a half-dozen different painting contractors come and go over the years.

Another painter quit painting interiors because too many customers claimed he had spilled paint on their rugs. Replacing the carpets for his dishonest customers cut into his profits.

"Everyone cheats," said Karen, 22, giving an example from her own life. She told of clipping product coupons for her employer, a drugstore owner in southern Florida. The manufacturers redeemed them, but the drugstore never actually sold the products. Karen said the scheme netted them both "a lot of money."

"I love the extra cash for the coupons," added Karen. "I'm glad I did it, although I was definitely afraid of getting caught and charged with fraud. But I think it's OK to cheat if no one gets hurt. Companies don't count."

Some people believe companies do count. More than 10 years ago Beverly, a former Girl Scout leader, collected discount coupons to raise money for her troop. "The store would give the scouts half of the total value of the coupons," she recalled, "and we didn't have to buy anything. But wasn't the store cheating? The money had to come from somewhere. I still feel bad about that."

Why do these things remain in our memories to bug us year after year? We go over the details just as we keep testing a sore tooth with our tongue. We fear we have failed in our commitment to live as God's children. We may tell our story again and again and finally ask God for forgiveness. Assured that we are forgiven through Christ, we can continue with greater determination to do what's right. But not everyone has such a commitment to integrity.

Fiddling on the Job

A book on blue-collar "fiddling" in England by Gerald Mars describes workers' fraud on their own companies as a way of livelihood. Fraud is defined as lying in order to cheat someone out of something.

On a new job, Mars reports in *Cheats at Work*, employees quickly learn how much fiddling, or cheating, is acceptable. "This 'training' may be given in a kidding tone," admits Mars, "but it only takes about six months to pass from the introduction to experienced fiddler."

Workers understand they must not report anyone else's fiddling. Also, they must not do too much or too little. A waitress, for example, undercharges diners, counting on larger tips as a reward. The customer doesn't pay any more, and the underpaid waitress makes more money. Only the unseen, faceless restaurant owner is cheated.

To sell copy machines, a salesperson carefully prepares for a demonstration before a company executive. He pays a middle-level manager to jam the rival copier, making its manufacturer look bad and his own good.

A supermarket checkout clerk rings up the wrong change to make herself some extra money on the job. "I just announce a lower amount, and no one notices," explained the fiddling clerk.

A journalist explains how he reports first-class travel costs on his "cheat sheet," but travels second class. He pockets the difference, rationalizing that "a good story deserves good expenses."

Only the company loses out, they say, and the company has plenty of money. What's the harm? they reason. A corporation is an impersonal and unfeeling entity. The losses from fiddling have become part of the expense of doing business—reflected in higher prices paid by consumers.

Giving away the Store

A full-blown swindler named Mr. Golspie is described in J. B. Priestley's 1930s novel, *Angel Pavement*. Mr. Golspie started work at the London offices of Twigg & Dersingham, sellers of wood veneers. He insisted upon a high commission, paid up front. With an exclusive supplier contact, Golspie quickly generated an enormous amount of business.

The "con man's" supplier, who was in on the scam, quoted low prices on high-quality veneers. Golspie wrote hundreds of orders before he absconded with his commissions.

The contact-supplier then raised his prices 70 percent. Twigg & Dersingham were now buying high and selling low.

"We've sold it, stacks and stacks of it, thousands of square feet, big orders, big orders, all those orders we paid Golspie that commission on," wailed Dersingham. "It's ruination. It's damnable unfair. We've simply been swindled."

Dersingham's wife, who never paid any attention to business before, saw her tranquil life vanishing. "But do you mean to say that brute has gone and you can't do anything, anything at all?" she asked. "But it's ridiculous. Can't you tell the police? Why, it's just as bad as burglary or swindling. It is swindling."

The effect of the caper on Mrs. Dersingham was intense: "She suddenly saw the four walls enclosing them, the table and chairs and sideboard, everything in sight, no longer as solid objects, fixed, rooted in a secure existence, but as things brittle as glass, unstable and wavering as water. . . . She realized now, with a shock of dismay, that something absurd and fantastic could happen in [her husband's office], far away, that could change all this. . . . All the cleaning and cooking and shopping and visiting, was a mere candle-flame—one puff of wind, a wind that came from nowhere, and it was gone. She understood how millions of people live. It was a moment of revelation."

And the culprit? He was standing on the deck of a ship, bound for Argentina, enjoying the sea spray and contemplating his next victim.

As victims, we are all interconnected with such examples of misconduct. Cheating is more than a news story describing some corporate swindle, to which we only give half of our attention. It's more than a kid cribbing in a math test, or a householder finagling a tax form. It is like a giant amoeba devouring all the facets of our lives.

Cheating is an umbrella word that encompasses forms of deceit from lying, fraud, and bribery to plagiarism and swindling. It also includes the betrayal of personal trust. Betrayal in a personal relationship may be the hardest for us to handle.

Questions for Reflection or Discussion

1. What has been your experience with cheating on the job? Do you know people who take home supplies (pens, lumber, whatever) or who do personal tasks (check writing, naps) on company time?

2. When in your life have you encountered "a deal too good to pass up"? Have you received mailings or phone calls that say you have won something, or could win something if you do as they say?

3. What can be done to prevent deceit in the workplace? Have you heard of any companies or groups who have done something to prevent cheating and to restore honesty?

3

Deceit and Throwaway Relationships

> *The woman said, "The serpent deceived me,*
> *and I ate."*
>
> —Genesis 3:13

"You're probably meeting your girlfriend." Sylvia spoke the familiar line in a monotone, unconcerned that the children were listening.

"Look, the boss is calling a Saturday meeting," Ed answered. "Do you think I like giving up my one free day?"

He couldn't convince his wife that he wasn't cheating on her. At dinner that night, Sylvia kept up the accusations, imagining her husband and his girlfriend eating lunch at a sidewalk cafe, followed by a romantic walk on the beach and then cocktails in his girlfriend's apartment. Even the children entered into the grilling, asking their father what his girlfriend looked like and if they would get to meet her.

"I don't know why you do this, Sylvia." Ed settled down with his headphones and stereo, and turned the volume up. "You're torturing all of us."

Fear of betrayal in a personal relationship is very real. Just the thought of infidelity causes panic. It's the first thing many people think of when they hear the word *cheating*. It's the first thing Sylvia thought of when her marriage was no longer happily-ever-after.

Are we looking for the perfect love that only God has shown us? If we're disappointed, like Sylvia, we feel helpless and lash out. In too many cases, betrayal itself is real.

Ever since Adam and Eve rejected the blame for bending some rules, men and women have lamented that they have been tricked, jilted, and rejected. They point a finger at any nearby culprit and tell their story to all who will listen. Country and western music abounds in you-done-me-wrong songs, such as "Your Cheatin' Heart" and "The Last Cheater's Waltz."

Stories of betrayal propel movies, romance novels, soap and grand operas, and literature. Sexual attraction and love seem to be dogged by dishonesty. The throw-away lover is as common as the Styrofoam coffee cup.

Betrayal of trust exists in great abundance in this world. We may wonder whether it is possible to experience both eros (sexual love) and agape (unconditional love). But God's love is a model of agape love for us. God can enable us to share agape love as well as sexual love with our spouses.

Hidden Contracts

We have to look at the problem from a number of perspectives. August Strindberg, in his 1885 short story "Cheated," argued that deceit is the very basis of relations between women and men. He said sexual deception begins with the "padding used by young, hopeful women" to emphasize their curves, and by men to broaden their manly shoulders.

Strindberg described a couple, preened and padded, engaged in a whirlwind courtship. A debt-ridden lieutenant, who was also a count, wooed the daughter of a prosperous wholesale dealer. The young lieutenant propositioned the woman *with his eyes only* in this way: "Will you pay my debts for me?"

With his lips, he asked, "Will you love me in fair weather and foul?"

She answered, *with her eyes*, "Yes, if you will make me your countess and introduce me into high society; if you will see that papa gets a chance to play cards with your generals and that mama becomes an intimate of your nobility; if you will provide for me for the rest of my days and let me enjoy life."

But when the father-in-law wholesaler went bankrupt, everything soured. There was no money for the lieutenant's creditors and nothing to maintain the newlyweds' social life. Feeling cheated, they divorced.

Was deceit the basis of their relationship, as Strindberg contended? Or can we narrow the problem down to an ignorance of each other's hidden contract, the messages conveyed only by their eyes?

Partners repeat sacred vows of allegiance. Usually they don't plan to dishonor their mate's trust but they may have secret scenarios, as did the lieutenant and the wholesaler's daughter.

Mystery Scripts

Lovers often see themselves as directors of their own show. The newly acquired partner is expected to follow some phantom script, sight unseen without a read-through or dress rehearsal. Many mates never even suspect there is a script other than the one in their own heads.

Jodie, a returning college student, was shocked to learn this hard lesson when her fiance said he didn't love her anymore. It was the same day that the 37-year-old woman discovered she was pregnant.

But Kevin wanted out. He was preoccupied with a previous, failed marriage and struggles with alcoholism. Jodie and he had met six months before at an Alcoholics Anonymous meeting when Kevin was new to the program.

As a veteran in the AA program, Jodie realized that Kevin's recent pledge to sobriety made him vulnerable to major commitments. Yet she ignored the warning signs. She was following her own scenario.

When I saw Jodie soon after she met Kevin, she was bubbling with happiness. "I'm really in love," she said. "I've never been in love like this, even though I was once married for 12 years." Jodie's red hair seemed to take flight in the light breeze. She was Boticelli's Venus.

"Kevin's never had children, either, so we're going to have a family," she continued. "I'm finally doing all the normal things—going to college, graduating, getting married, and having babies." She laughed at her rate of progression. "I'm just a little slower than most."

Her long-delayed education was to be the prelude to an exciting advertising career. When she and Kevin became engaged, she had enthusiastically included marriage and having a family in her future. They made starry-eyed plans. Suddenly he zigged and she zagged. The time sequence went awry. She faced single motherhood one month after graduating from college.

In the early depths of Jodie's dilemma, she came to my house for lunch one day. "I've considered abortion," she said. "In fact, that's what my mother says I should do."

Jodie continued talking, bringing in all the pros and cons but constantly returning to two themes: "I really want a child, and time is running out for me."

Her sense of humor returned. "You know, when I used to pray for God's help I would add, 'but don't make me *average.'* That's dangerous stuff. As you can see, this is no average mess."

Then a friend offered Jodie a place to stay until the baby arrived. A three-day-a-week internship job at an ad agency helped Jodie meet expenses. Jodie was determined to handle the birth and rearing of the child alone.

Tradition of Betrayal

Betrayal of trust is a timeless story, repeated in every culture. Secret scenarios are only part of the problem. We also live in communities that are less than perfect, where betrayal may be a tradition.

Society often sanctions deceitful attitudes. Colleagues at the office openly discuss various alliances, neighbors gossip at the shopping mall, and friends trade jokes and sly looks. Who has been seen together and who has been discarded—it's all part of today's small talk, along with the weather and sports news.

Young people are quick to see these changes in society. Relationships are no longer seen as long-standing, inviolate alliances. The throwaway lover has become a tradition.

A national study showed that 70 to 80 percent of those responding believed that extramarital relations were wrong. But half of the respondents admitted they had participated in such relations anyway. If this survey is representative, it means that more than one-third of the population is cheating on their spouses.

People use affairs just as an alcoholic uses alcohol, says Dr. Jennifer Schneider in her book, *Back from Betrayal.* Both partners, the betrayed and the betrayer, become trapped in an addictive system.

Marriage today is making new demands. The Rev. Larry Burton, an ethics teacher at the Kantor Family Institute in Cambridge, Mass., says mates who stray "are reasserting ambivalence about commitment . . . to get 'distance.' "

Burton sees tension between a partner who is guided only by personal feelings and a mate who practices compromise and forgiveness. The traditional "you-firster" marries the "me-firster."

"A conflict arises," Burton says, "when people's assumptions and ways of dealing with ethical questions are not the same." Similar to the hidden-contract problem, differing values call for negotiation.

Yet too many important issues are never brought up between partners, writes Ellen Steese in an April 8, 1988, article in the *Christian Science Monitor*. For example, the question of needs should be hashed out between lovers, she thinks, before they get too serious. They should discuss the personal needs of each partner, and also the collective needs of the two of them as a couple.

"Will my needs jeopardize the relationship?" is a good question to be addressed, Steese suggests. Another is: "How open shall I be about my personal longings?"

A Litany of Hurts

Real communication could help those who are looking for answers to the betrayed relationship. Many of them are hurting. Ray presented a diamond ring to Trish, insisting that she "keep it as a token of my love even if the answer is no." When she did just that, he was bitter.

For no reason that Bo could see, her husband strayed next door. "Two years later," she said, "I am forlorn and alone, like a little girl who has lost her mother."

George said his efforts to provide for his family went unappreciated, so he felt justified to "try sex with a prostitute while on a business trip." His wife would never know.

George visited a massage parlor in New York City and said he felt curious and queasy. "I would probably have felt very guilty if I had brought a sexually transmitted disease back to my wife. But there was no caring between the prostitute and me—a lack of real sexual interest. [The experience] was nearly totally unsatisfactory."

Friends and neighbors can tell sad variations of these themes. Can we place the blame on eroded values and traditions? Is the problem in hidden contracts between partners? Does the relationship lack openness, or has there been too much?

Some couples have tried an open marriage, arguing that it was the honest solution. There can't be any betrayal, they claim, if there is no trust to begin with.

Henry, who lives in Kentucky with his wife, Gretchen, agreed to an open arrangement. He said he and Gretchen both travel in their work and this gives them "many opportunities to cheat. I mostly do it because I love women, and making love. I keep an apartment just for such meetings.

"I have never counted the women I've been with. In the last four years, women have started to ask me first, sometimes out of the blue. I've run the gamut from women I truly loved, to one-night stands over which I felt guilty for wasting my time and risking my health."

Henry admitted feelings of revenge and inferiority that may have influenced his choice of life-style. He regretted the time that his affairs took away from his children. He also said he and his wife no longer love each other. He doesn't care for her boyfriends, either. "One of Gretchen's lovers was a jerk, and they flaunted their affair in front of me. That was a problem."

Eventually Henry found too many problems in their open marriage. Closed, monogamous relationships can be troublesome, too, fraught with misunderstandings and suffering. What is the basis for honest personal relationships?

To find honest love, we can hold up God's love as a model. We can count on the love we receive from God. Scripture teaches that God's love led him to send his son whose life, death, and resurrection assure us that nothing can separate us from God's love (Rom. 8:38, 39). Christ has shown us the perfect life. He is the light, leading us out of darkness.

God has also sent us the Holy Spirit to empower us to share God's love with our neighbors. By living lives of neighborly love we can begin to overcome dishonesty in our world and in our relationships.

Love is eternal, Paul explained in 1 Corinthians 13. "Love is patient, love is kind. It does not envy, it does not boast, it is not proud. It is not rude, it is not self-seeking, it is not easily angered, it keeps no record of wrongs. Love does not delight in evil but rejoices with truth. It always protects, always trusts, always hopes, always perseveres."

If we can follow what the Bible teaches us about loving our neighbors, our relationships will have more integrity. We can reveal any hidden contracts we might have. We can examine traditional assumptions and values when our relationships are honest. We can talk to our loved ones and express ourselves. We can listen and really hear.

If we see our fellow human beings as Christ sees them, we will want to help them, not injure them. Jesus taught that by feeding the hungry, giving the thirsty a drink of cold water, welcoming the stranger, clothing the naked, and comforting those who are sick or in prison, we are doing those actions for Jesus (Matt. 25:34). And in Matt. 18:20 we learn that Christ is present when we gather in his name. With this understanding, we will care about others' feelings as much as we care about our own. We won't want to hurt another person any more than we would want to be hurt. We will look out for our partner just as we look out for ourselves.

The me-firsters can become us-firsters. Tapping into God's love, we can share loving concern for each other.

Still, we won't always know exactly what to do in each situation in life, but we know that God is guiding us. God's Spirit often speaks in the form of our conscience. What do we know about this powerful presence? How well do we listen to this inner voice?

Questions for Reflection or Discussion

1. When readers first see this book's title, some of them think it is only about husbands cheating on their wives and vice versa. Do you think that kind of cheating is more common now than it was 50 years ago? Why or why not?

2. The author talks about hidden contracts, pp. 36-37. Why are they so destructive? What keeps people from honestly saying what their expectations are?

3. To what extent do TV programs and movies affect our ideas about relationships between men and women? Which programs promote good examples?

PART 2
Looking at All Sides

4

What about Conscience?

The guilty soul says, "I can't hide from God."
The witness of the gospel is,
"You don't have to!"
—Fortress Weekly Church Bulletins, Mar. 24, 1989

The laundromat had been deserted the whole time Ellen was there that evening. She was bundling up her fluff-dried clothes and looking once more at the nearly full bottle of Downy that sat on the folding table.

Nobody's going to come back for that now, Ellen thought. It's almost closing time. The softener might as well be mine, instead of someone else's tomorrow.

The gray-haired grandmother of four tightened the lid on the bottle, put it in her basket, and drove home. When she turned into her driveway, she stayed in her car for a few minutes. "I decided to go back," she recalled. "I couldn't bring that softener into my home. It didn't belong to me. I returned the bottle, right where it had been."

Was it fear of getting caught that made Ellen go back? She had a clear shot at getting away with it, and she could save a few dollars on her grocery bill. No one had seen her; no one would know. What sent her back?

Something very real to Ellen kept her from getting out of her car until she did the honest thing. An inner voice caught her attention. She listened and she obeyed her conscience.

Conscience at Work

How does our conscience work? What is it? The New Testament contains more than 30 references to the conscience. Paul said he was proud, in 2 Corinthians 1:12, that "our conscience testifies that we have conducted ourselves . . . in the holiness and sincerity that are from God." In Romans 9:1, Paul asserted that his conscience confirmed in the Holy Spirit that he was speaking the truth, not lies.

False teachings, wrote Timothy in 1 Timothy 4:2, "come through hypocritical liars, whose consciences have been seared as with a hot iron." The Bible talks about a weak conscience, a good conscience, and a clear conscience. A good conscience can be a great help in a dishonest world.

The conscience is our mediator in moral decisions, said Dr. James Knight in his book, *Conscience and Guilt*. More than that, he wrote, our conscience is the essence of our being. Instead of saying that we have a conscience, Knight suggested, it would be more accurate to say that we *are* one.

But there's no unanimous agreement about how this inner voice works, wrote Walter Conn in *Conscience: Development and Self-transcendence*. He said human beings have argued about it since Grecian civilization, or maybe longer.

Different cultures' approaches to deceit affect the conscience in different ways. Anthropologists tell us that the Somoans teach their children to lie well so they won't get caught. No small, quiet voice is going to bother the Somoan child after telling a successful lie. Believing that clever dishonesty is a good thing, the child would have a clear conscience.

There is a legend that newborn babies contain the wisdom of the ages and already know right from wrong. An angel seals their lips immediately, the story goes, and they have to learn it all over again. A child's conscience needs to be shaped.

Freud said that small children are amoral (without moral principles). Their conscience is influenced by the concept of honesty they pick up from parents and peers.

Psychologist Erik Erikson said a child's first year is the time to learn basic trust. Gradually children develop a notion of right and wrong. He placed the development of a conscience between the ages of 3 and 6. But not all children are pointed toward honesty. So much depends on how they are raised.

A Starved Conscience

Dick, a TV repairman in a Minneapolis suburb, had an upbringing that steered him in the wrong direction. His mother didn't seem to like him, he said, and constantly warned that he would turn out like his father.

"But I didn't know my father," Dick said, "so I didn't understand what she meant." He learned later that his father was an escaped convict, eventually hanged at Leavenworth, Kan.

Dick's family were carnies; his mother was the woman sawed in half and the "woman without a head." They once had a mother-and-son act, being shot out of a cannon together. That was as close as Dick ever got to his mother.

When Dick was five his uncle tried to teach him to pick pockets, but "I didn't have a light enough touch. I was beaten a lot and when I was eleven I was locked in a closet. My older sister, Gilda, guarded the door and I threatened to kill her.

"My step-brother, Barry, was four years older than me, and my step-Dad's favorite. When I made Eagle Scout the same time as Barry, I was smacked for it.

"So I just numbed my feelings, figuring some day they would accept me. I kept on trying to get love and attention."

Dick recalled that he was only 13 years old when he started stealing cars. His first arrest, at age 15, was for stealing a '52 4-door Chevy. "Can you straighten up?" the judge asked him.

"I just said, 'I don't know,' so I was sent to a home for boys, something like day care." Now bearded and rotund, and never far from his pack of cigarettes and can of beer, Dick guffaws at the idea of being cared for in that home. "I rebelled there, too. I just figured I would do better next time and not get caught."

There was no inner, or outer, voice telling him it was wrong to steal. He got away with robbing several banks. However, he eventually was nabbed for counterfeiting, running moonshine, and smuggling bogus FBI badges out of a prison print shop, among other crimes. All told, he served 12 years in prison.

During Dick's 1961 prison stay, he endured 97 days of isolation. "I had no light except for twice a day when they brought me toast and coffee. I was naked as a jay bird and had a cold concrete floor to sleep on. I kept myself sane by building a fantasy world in my mind. It was like reading a sci-fi book. I dreamed about outer space and I taught myself to do handstands and back flips. In the army I had learned karate and meditation for relieving pain. All of that helped."

Dick's inner spirit was awakening. In 1974, after two years in the Federal Correctional Institution in Sandstone, Minnesota, Dick "saw the light" and turned around 180 degrees. Even a new wife who wanted to live out a Bonnie and Clyde fantasy could not persuade him to go back to crime. "I finally got to thinking: No matter what I do they will eventually get me. I can't wear these bars out. Why not enjoy life? I wanted regular stuff, like sitting here on this deck and talking—swimming, a job. That would be a refreshing change."

He says he never felt remorse and doesn't believe in rehabilitation. Yet after 30 years God was able to reach him, to begin to work in his life. Dick became convinced that he was not meant to live the way he had been living.

A lack of conscience among prisoners is common, wrote Elwood, an inmate at the California state prison in Vacaville. He said most of the men there do not realize that "they have cheated their victims, families, society and above all, themselves."

In his letter, Elwood emphasized that "people who commit crimes are cheaters . . . and have a lack of self-esteem. Cheaters are also deniers, rationalizers, justifiers, excusers. . . ." He did not reveal the form of cheating that cost him a prison term, but said he was a former psychology teacher at a California university.

Freud said that some people don't have enough conscience. Many of them get away with dishonesty and never get caught and never feel guilty. We can wonder, however, if they have hidden problems that will surface years down the road. Will a developed conscience cry out later on? Will these people be looking for a chance to confess?

A Nagging Conscience

Taxpayers who pay up after 20 years of evasion often say their conscience hurt all those years. They could not rest until they did the honest thing.

One man, who claimed nine dogs as dependents on his tax return, quickly admitted his deceit when questioned. An IRS agent once asked an "18-dependents" man about his wife, and the man blurted out, "I'm not married, and I don't have any children, let alone 17 of them."

A criminal escaping from a serious crime often becomes a traffic offender. The getaway driver spots a traffic cop, drives erratically, and is finally pulled over for a traffic violation. Is this the work of his conscience?

An English surveyor said he never cheated in school, but with his trade exams it was different. These tests involved Guy's future career, his standing with superiors, and his income.

Guy scratched answers on clear plastic protractors with a compass point and he indented pencils with information. "I preferred to put my cribs on unexpected articles so I wouldn't be caught," he said. "It tested my ingenuity in the art of cheating. My favorite was inscribing notes on chewing gum."

Greed was his motivation, Guy admitted, but, "I am not overly ambitious. I am now quite content to be district surveyor, and will stay there."

Are we really content when we've "gotten away with it" or does something tell us that's enough deceit? The conscience can speak to us in many ways—intellectually and physically.

The changes in our body may be as subtle as a different look in the eyes, a line of perspiration on the upper lip, or a faint blush on the cheeks. The changes may be more severe. A man cheated his sister out of her inheritance, reported author James Knight in *Conscience and Guilt*, but suffered from chronic stomach pain until he relinquished her share.

Another case involves a woman complaining of periodic bouts with a bleeding ulcer. The flare-ups coincided with times she was cheating on her husband. Her behavior,

Knight concluded, violated her inner sense of right and wrong.

No User's Manual

How can we strengthen our conscience? We need to recognize that our conscience may be weak, undeveloped, or pushed aside. We also need to accept the fact that at first we won't understand its message. But the more we practice listening for God's direction, the clearer the message from our conscience will be. Just as we need aerobics or some kind of exercise for physical fitness, we need Bible study, devotional reading, and prayer for spiritual fitness. Being open to God's Spirit of love strengthens our consciences and gives us peace and reassurance.

"The only guide I have confidence in," wrote Jerald F. terHorst, former press secretary for President Ford, "is personal conscience, that internal reminder of our basic beliefs and ethical values."

When Ford gave ex-President Nixon a complete pardon, terHorst resigned, believing the pardon was unjust. He said he has never regretted his decision. Politics can have principles, he contends.

Your conscience can overrule misguided loyalty. But when it points you in a definite direction, consider your actions carefully. Try to imagine the consequences. Then look at the exact opposite approach. Consider, in either case, who will be hurt and who will be helped. What do you think Christ would do?

Looking at these different approaches will help you test the message. Was it wishful thinking, some kind of a cop-out, or your conscience speaking? A conscience doesn't come with directions. Yours might even be overactive and out of control.

Some people have a merciless conscience that rages at every perceived slip from perfection. Dr. Knight told of a student who continually shaded her eyes with her hand during school tests. She said she couldn't allow any chance that she might read an answer from another student's paper.

Once she wrote a note in the margin of her exam, confessing that she may have gleaned one idea from her neighbor. She also admitted that when her fellow students were whispering, she had overhead a few words. That same semester this young woman won an oratory medal but almost gave it back. She wasn't sure she had abided by all the rules.

We can see that this is an extreme case. We don't want to drag along such guilty baggage with us through exams, relationships, or life. In searching for a better balance, we can be alert to misgivings that masquerade as our conscience. We can weigh them according to the situation. We may need to talk with our family, minister, colleagues, boss, or teacher about the situation and compare standards. Then we have to come to our own, honest conclusions.

As a university instructor who orders about 100 textbooks every semester for my classes, I receive free books from publishers who want to influence my choice. After five years I had a stack of about 20 such textbooks, most of them stamped "Complimentary copy" and "Not for resale."

When a publisher's rep asked to buy these books from me, I was surprised. I decided to check with some other people on campus. The department secretary told me it was unethical to sell the books. A respected science prof said he sold his complimentary books but used the money to purchase publications he really needed.

A professor new to the campus pointed out to me that the authors of these books are cheated out of royalties if books are resold in this way. However, he said, the books are resold at a discount to students. "So it helps the students," he added, "as well as us underpaid teachers."

He gave me the phone number of the representative with whom he dealt. Now I'm trying to come to an honest conclusion, as the books sit in two stacks in the corner of my loft.

A Confessing Conscience

Because I know I'm like the imperfect clay pots Paul wrote about in 2 Corinthians, I might make the wrong decision, but nevertheless will endure. Our flaws, Paul pointed out, give us strength. I can acknowledge my error, accept God's forgiveness, and go on with my life.

Just as we teach our children to tell the truth when they've done something wrong, we have to do the same. If our child has to admit breaking a playmate's favorite little truck, we have to confess that we ate the last muffin, or wrongly sold a complimentary textbook. Confession, or admission, is the first step in clearing a guilty conscience.

In this electronic age, there's a telephone hotline helping people to confess if they feel the need. Every day several hundred people telephone "Ms. Apology," part of California-based United Communications International. Ms. Apology's soothing voice encourages the caller to tell all, at the rate of $2 for one minute and $.45 for each additional minute.

Who calls? One man said, "I'm sorry I hurt Grace and got her pregnant. We used to love each other and now she's moving away. I would like to say I'm sorry."

A woman apologized to Richard: "I know you ran around with other women, so I went to bed with your brother. When you found out, you were hurt. Please forgive me."

A 17-year-old said he's leaving home as soon as he's 18 because he's been unhappy for the last three years. "My parents say they wish they had never had me. That I've screwed up all my life. I hope things will be better on my own."

That's all there is to it. The callers receive no answer. No counseling. No therapy. But their message can be heard the next day. By dialing a special number, Grace can hear her ex-boyfriend's apology, Richard hears his girlfriend's confession, and the teenager's parents can listen to his explanation. The high-tech messages are once-removed from the individual.

Detractors have dubbed the service "cry and run" or supermarket therapy. "It's so sad, really," said M. J. Denton, the voice of Ms. Apology. "I care about these people. But what does this say about our society—that people can't talk to each other?"

The need is there to unload, whether we're caught in a misdeed, getting away with it, or a victim. Counseling with our pastor, confessing to a priest or rabbi, or taking part in a family complaint session or neighborly "gripe" over coffee, can help us deal with this instinct to mend fences.

But not everyone has sympathetic friends and family nearby. We may have no spiritual leader to turn to, or we don't know how to pray for guidance and forgiveness. We are left with a telephone service to soothe a guilty conscience.

The important step is admitting our error. Then we are more likely to be open to God's love. Remember, much of our conscience is God's voice within us—not a ranting, raving, accusing bellow but a still, small voice.

Although our conscience is our guide, it is fragile, dependent on nurturing input from outside sources and recognition by us. Taking part in discussion groups, adult Sunday school classes, and conversations with close friends about spiritual matters can tone up your conscience. Bible study, prayer, and meditation can put you in touch with the Holy Spirit who can guide your conscience. A healthy conscience is neither a deafening nag nor a whimper that is too easily ignored. As you practice your honesty, nudge your conscience constantly. You need your conscience when life events put you to the test in difficult matters.

For example, how well can your conscience handle special circumstances? What if you are facing a unique situation that isn't clearly honest or dishonest, no matter how you look at it? A problem may be a just-this-once exception to all your instincts of integrity.

Will your conscience allow you to cheat? In fact, is it ever ethical to be dishonest or to break the law?

Questions for Reflection or Discussion

1. Is it dishonest to take something that apparently was abandoned (e.g. a piece of camping equipment in a remote area)?

2. Do you know of anyone who, years after a theft or dishonest action, finally confessed?

3. Is it possible to have too sensitive a conscience so that a person is always apologizing and worrying about offending? Do you know any people like that?

4. How can you help your conscience be active yet balanced (not too hard on you and not too easygoing)?

5

Are There Good Reasons to Cheat?

Love with care, and then do
what you will.
—St. Augustine

A surprise $6,000 refund from the IRS startled Karl, a Los Angeles engineer. Checking his records, he could see that the refund was an error by the tax office. "I couldn't keep the money once I knew that it wasn't rightly mine," the middle-aged aerospace executive said. "I just couldn't rest, knowing that."

Karl wrote a letter to the IRS, explaining the situation. They thanked him for pointing out the mistake and asked for the money back. Karl sent off the check.

Next he received a computerized bill from the IRS office asking him to pay $6,190—$190 in interest, plus the $6,000. There was no acknowledgment that he had already returned $6,000.

Karl complained. Finally, the IRS office told him they had found the $6,000 check he had returned. Still, they insisted on the interest due.

Karl could've dug in his heels for a long, drawn-out battle over the $190, or he could've given up and paid the interest. If he had known in advance about these hassles, wouldn't he have just kept the $6,000? But he couldn't keep it. Even if the IRS seemed inept, he had no reason to cheat.

Exceptional Exceptions

Are there exceptions when we can truly say that it's OK to cheat or lie? Are there extenuating circumstances? I believe there are and we must be prepared to meet them.

Reva, a housewife with twin sons in junior high, believes in a strict code of honesty. She is teaching her children to always tell the truth. However, she acted surprisingly out of character during a neighborhood crisis.

The doorbell rang. Reva saw it was Carol from next door, the neighbor with junk piled in her side yard. The two women usually didn't see much of each other.

Carol immediately started talking. "Can I stay here for a while? I'm so mixed up. When I saw it was four o'clock and that Mitch would be home in a half-hour, I had to get out of the house. I didn't even take my purse. But I can't go back. He might come home while I'm there. And I can't stand it any longer. He goes into a rage sometimes and I'm afraid of what's going to happen. I've never told this to anyone before."

As the two women sat on the couch, Carol poured forth a story of beatings and mental anguish during the past 20 years. Reva was shocked. She had always thought better of Mitch, maybe because he often apologized for the junk in the yard and promised to remove it and cut down the weeds, too.

Reva didn't know what she should do. Her own family would be coming home for dinner soon. She had a PTA meeting that night. What would be the right thing to do? She didn't know whether to believe Carol or not. Wasn't there some kind of battered-women's shelter in town?

Reva's boys came in the front door. They said "Hi" as they glanced at Carol, who was crying. They headed for the kitchen and Reva was about to follow them, saying she had to start dinner, when she was startled by pounding on the front door.

"That's Mitch." Carol slumped back into the corner of the sofa, whimpering.

The pounding got louder. The boys were in the hall-way now, holding half-eaten sandwiches as they stared at the door, and then at their mother.

Reva stood up. "Carol, go into my bedroom and close the door. Boys, back to the kitchen."

Waiting until everyone was out of sight, Reva opened the front door. It was Mitch. "Where's my wife?"

"Why?" Reva was afraid she couldn't fool Mitch. "Why do you ask?"

"Oh, I don't know." Mitch laughed and put his hands in his jeans pockets. "She sure isn't at home."

"I've been so busy all day," Reva answered, "I haven't been paying attention." She could hear her boys, chewing and swallowing their peanut-butter sandwiches, a few yards behind her.

Mitch looked at her closely. "You haven't seen Carol?"

Reva took a deep breath and looked at the man directly. "No, not all day."

"You sure?"

"Yes, I'm sure."

Reva surprised herself with her story telling. She hadn't done much of it since the age of eight when she had fibbed to her mother about a gumball she took from the dime store.

Mitch turned on his heel and left without another word. She watched him get into his pickup truck and roar down the street. Her boys came toward her.

"Why did you tell him that?" one boy asked. "What's going on?"

Reva sent them back to the kitchen. She knew her sons were more shocked by her fib than by knowing a neighbor woman was hiding in their house. Somehow she would try to explain later, but at the time she was sure she had done the right thing.

This was different than lying about a gumball. Later that night she heard how Mitch had driven his pickup truck through town in a rampage, breaking off several signposts. Reva was able to convince her sons that this was an exception; a time when it was OK to lie.

A Risky Business

Sometimes there may be a higher standard than a legalistic form of honesty. Honesty depends on the many facets of each situation. We see the right thing to do, even if it goes against our usual principles of honesty, and we do it.

But it can be risky. We might be wrong. A social worker in Sacramento, California, felt awful after she bent a few rules and lied to an inspector.

Peggy Nickerson said she thought she was helping provide shelter for the homeless by evading some of the system's red tape. The social worker had sent a dozen of her "misfit" clients to a new boardinghouse she had just discovered. She ignored warning signs and safeguards.

The place turned out to be the final stop for several hapless clients. They were murdered by the landlady for their government checks.

"I have that hurting, stinging feeling in my stomach," Nickerson said as she reviewed the case. "I was trying to protect my clients. I thought they would at least have a place to stay. I don't like the idea of people being thrown out on the street."

She thought she saw a higher good that would cancel out the wrong she did. Instead she made a fatal mistake. Now the guilt she feels won't leave.

How can we know when to go around the laws or codes? Isn't this shaky ground? Wouldn't it be easier just to follow the rules, blindly? Yes, but we have to leave the door open—even if it's only a crack.

The Bible tells about people who felt compelled to follow a higher law. In Acts 4:18-20, Peter and John defied the authorities who commanded them not to speak or teach in the name of Jesus. The two replied, "Judge for yourselves whether it is right in God's sight to obey you rather than God."

The commandment that immediately follows Jesus' Great Commandment to love the Lord with our whole being is the one that says we are to love our neighbor as ourselves (Matt. 22:37-39). We have to carefully consider the best ways we can do that. Will anyone be hurt by our actions, and who will be helped? We can try to see long-range repercussions as well as immediate results. Sometimes we must decide quickly and we may make mistakes. But God is with us, guiding us and also assuring us that through Christ we live in God's forgiveness and love.

Reva went against her code to tell the truth. Doing so, she saved a neighbor from a beating, or worse. German theologian Dietrich Bonhoeffer called this kind of situational decision "responsible action." He saw it as a way of showing love of God and neighbor.

Following a strict code of always telling the truth would be a "case of self-righteousness of conscience," said Bonhoeffer. Such absolutism would follow all rules, ignoring the exceptional situation that dictates love over the law.

It All Depends

Jesus did not legalistically obey all the laws of his day, but rather followed higher laws. For instance, on the Sabbath

Jesus healed the man with the withered hand (Matt. 12:9-14). He went against the rules forbidding work on that day. He did it again when he allowed his disciples to eat by picking grain on the Sabbath (Matt. 12:1-2).

Jesus' concern for helping people overrode the rules. He told complainers around him that God wants us to show each other kindness; the Sabbath was made for people, not the other way around.

Love takes precedence over law when the law has become loveless. "When the law impels one against love," said Martin Luther in one of his sermons, "it ceases and should no longer be law . . . if (the law) cannot be kept without injury to the neighbor, God wants us to suspend and ignore the law."

When we care about someone else's health, happiness, and well-being, we may have to turn our backs on a legalistic approach. Mark Twain's Huckleberry Finn dealt with nagging worries that he should report Jim, the escaped slave, to the authorities.

The two of them were floating down the Mississippi River on a raft, and Huck knew that Jim belonged to a woman in Hannibal. Jim was the woman's property and represented a sizable investment to her. Jim told Huckleberry he was planning to steal his children from the slave owners who had bought them.

Huck knew the law backed the slave owners, but he decided to follow a higher principle. He was living up to an ideal of human dignity, carried deep within himself.

Does that mean we can do whatever we feel like? Have we just been sent off to follow our whims? Do we agree that if it feels good, do it—that sort of thing? Hardly.

Paul wrote about this in 1 Corinthians 6:12. He said that someone might say, " 'Everything is permissible for me'—but not everything is beneficial. 'Everything is permissible for me'—but I will not be mastered by anything."

The Greater Good

We have been given freedom, balanced by responsibility. Making the right decisions about honesty requires mature judgment, the weighing of consequences, and loving concern for the people involved. We choose the *lesser evil* to produce the *greater good*.

In 1849, Harriet Tubman managed to escape from a Maryland slave plantation. Burdened by the plight of her brothers and sisters, she became a leader in the underground railroad, which helped slaves escape to the North. She disobeyed the law, first by fleeing her owner and then by helping more than 300 slaves to escape. She saw a greater good and felt called by God to take action against unjust laws. Her nickname captures that idea; she was called "the Moses of her people."

Another person who disobeyed the law for a greater good was Corrie Ten Boom. As she and her family watched Nazi forces round up Jewish families and haul them away, they knew they had to do something. In defiance of the law and at great danger to themselves, they hid Jews in their home and helped them escape. The Ten Booms had experienced the love of God and sought to live in accordance with that love, regardless of the laws of their day.

Children Watch Their Parents

Psychologist Lawrence Kohlberg said that very young children operate under a code called "infant legalism." Toddlers and preschoolers like rules and expect everyone to follow them exactly. Eventually children leave this kind of absolutism behind for a more flexible truth. Dietrich Bonhoeffer said children learn the "it depends" style from observing their parents, who demand truth from them but do not reciprocate.

Too many parents have their children study church doctrine that they themselves do not follow. Moms and dads make unkept promises to go swimming, manipulate unwelcome guests, and crow over their ability to "put one over" on an unpopular neighbor.

They often give these kinds of directives:

- Tell Aunt Mathilda you love the socks she gave you for Christmas.
- I want you to look happy when Daddy's boss arrives.
- Don't give me that bored look.
- We'll get a half-price ticket and say you're only 11.

The Social Cover-up

Children have only a few options to respond to parents' unrealistic commands, said J. Barton Bowyer in his book, *Cheating*. They can submit, run away, rebel, or cheat. In extreme cases, children will even commit suicide.

Children cheat to protect themselves, to avoid punishment or chores, and to win unwarranted praise. Some also find a thrill in outwitting others.

In the grown-up world, these are not considered legitimate reasons to cheat. As children mature, they learn to discern when total honesty is not necessary for their purposes.

Psychologist Esther Greenglass, York University, Ontario, Canada, has studied children's willingness to tell what she calls "an altruistic lie" (*Journal of Genetic Psychology*, Dec. 1972). A so-called accidental breaking of a vase was the setting for Greenglass's experiment.

The assumed culprit had previously given grades to the artwork created by the children in the test. Now the "grader" was asking the children to cover up the accident in case they should be questioned about it.

Greenglass found that eight-year-olds were reluctant to tell this altruistic, cover-up lie. But most of the 12-year-old subjects were quite willing to lie, especially if the "culprit" had given them a good grade on their artwork. They simply were reciprocating and returning the favor.

Children learn to lie for social survival. Adults tell their little white lies an average of 13 times a week, or about twice a day, according to a study described in *Glamour*. The article encouraged its readers to go ahead and lie because of the pressures of modern-day "overload."

The advise was to rationalize and to give convincing excuses: "Don't feel guilty. Everyone needs a mental-health break now and then. People understand. They've told a few white lies, too."

We can all think of examples of our own or others' white lies. For instance, Susan may say she can't help stuff envelopes this morning at the church because she has an appointment with her doctor. Actually her appointment is in the afternoon. Frank may say no to helping a neighbor move, claiming his back is giving him trouble when it's been fine for more than a year. Are those white lies OK? Doesn't everybody, even very honest people, tell some white lies sometimes?

We have to face these issues of honesty and occasional dishonesty, especially in raising our children. Do we tell them that white lies are OK? If we say "sometimes," then how do we explain *when* they are OK?

Graying the White Lie

One way to look at your personal fibbing score is to look at your motivation and at your frequency of bending the truth. Are 13 white lies a week about average for you, and do you see any trends? Are you always telling your husband that he's right, even when he isn't? Is your motivation to give him confidence, or peace at any price, or some other reason?

Did you laud your neighbor's cooking so she would take charge of the Scout dinner, or do you really think she's a great chef? Are you protecting a friend's feelings, or saving your own skin. Maybe the little white lie is not so little or so white anymore.

But sometimes there seems to be no alternative to lying. Suppose you had to cover up for your boss to keep your job. What if your boss were the president of the company, or the president of the United States?

How about lying to save someone's life or reputation? Is it OK to cheat one person to save 100? What about cheating 100 to save 10?

Only you can answer these questions for yourself, depending on the circumstances. And you will have to look at each situation carefully and consider the dilemmas that exist.

That's the beginning of awareness. You build on that reality with the concept of loving concern. Consider who will be hurt and who will benefit.

The important point is to realize that there are difficulties with being an absolute legalist. This is a lesson to be carefully taught to our children.

Corrie Ten Boom put love above the law and saved the lives of many Jewish people. Huck Finn struggled with his conscience at first, then felt comfortable helping his runaway-slave friend. Harriet Tubman, herself a slave, clearly saw the need to obey a higher law as she worked with the underground railroad.

The social worker's conscience hurt because of a wrong decision, even though her mistake was motivated by loving concern. She will probably never forget what happened, but she can't quit trying to do the best she can. If she will accept God's free forgiveness through Christ, she has a clean slate to go on with life.

Reva showed her sons that she puts another person's well-being over her code of always telling the truth. Karl's code of honesty forced him to send back a $6000 windfall and will probably cost him another $190. He feels a clear conscience is worth it.

These exceptional examples can be applied to daily decisions you face. When you do bypass or overrule a law or standard, you need to understand the consequences, both spiritual and temporal. You must be clear about your concern for a higher principle when you make exceptions.

But most of all, you need to know all the powerful reasons *not* to bend the rules. You must know your own scriptural and personal codes of integrity intimately.

Writer Martin Buber said a lie is possible only after we understand what is true. If you're going to say that sometimes it's OK to cheat, you better have a firm grasp on what it means to be honest.

Questions for Reflection or Discussion

1. Think of examples when some sort of dishonesty (such as lying to a thief who is looking for valuables in your house) may be "a lesser evil for a greater good."

2. What might parents try to teach their children to do that the parents themselves don't do? Has that ever happened in your family?

3. The author refers to people breaking the law when a system was unjust, as when slavery was legal. Are there issues in society today that might lead conscientious people to break the law?

PART 3
Facing the Problem

6

Why Should I Be Honest?

Dale could see the answers on a fellow student's paper at the next desk. He turned away and looked out the window. An elm tree was leafing out after the warm spell the day before. He looked again at Barbara Soderberg's test. She would have the right answers, those formulas that had gone completely out of his head.

But what is one exam? Dale asked himself. There are more important things than passing this test, even more important than getting good grades or graduating from high school.

Humorist Garrison Keillor told us in *Lake Wobegon Days* that the Minnesota teenager put down his pencil and ignored Barbara Soderberg's right answers. "Life is so wonderful," Dale decided. "It's almost all we need. We don't need to lie and cheat."

That's a good reason for us to be honest, isn't it? God intends us to have a wonderful life and to be happy and fulfilled. That's what we were created for—to live in harmony with ourselves, our neighbors, and God. Honesty and integrity are God's will for his children, and an honest and corruption-free society is a place of peace and well-being. As Christians we know that even if others around us lie and cheat, we don't need to. Instead, each of us can be an honest beacon, like a light on a hill for our neighbors.

There are other reasons for honesty. Your own self-respect is important. And you are a role model, not only for your family and friends but for people in your neighborhood you don't even know. Community values need constant attention. You may have to prop them up occasionally through example.

A friend sidled up to me at a busy fast-food salad bar and asked me to put something on my tray for her. Since she hadn't paid for the salad bar, she couldn't help herself to the melon or the apple she wanted.

I put a couple of melon wedges on my tray and a big, red apple. Although I didn't feel right about it, I did it anyway. I pledged to myself that next time I would refuse.

But does it really matter? It's easier to comply than to make a scene. After all, what are a few pieces of fruit? I have to remind myself that this practice at salad bars might have something to do with increasing pilferage in grocery stores.

At the market, I see children and their mothers snacking as they shop, tasting cookies, fruit, and candy—on the house. If taking one grape is OK, then so are two, and on and on and on. Would the food samplers steal the goods in a toy store, or gift shop? Or salad bar? I resolve that there will be no extra apples on my tray next time.

Looking Up at Yourself

Personal integrity is a precious commodity. "Once integrity goes," said the arch-villain J. R. Ewing on TV's "Dallas," "the rest is a piece of cake." This is a powerful reason for honesty, one to remember when in doubt. Madge learned this lesson after a bitter experience.

Madge looked at her son over the morning paper want-ads. She was happy that he was back home again, but she still worried about him.

Troy adjusted his baseball cap and raised one eyebrow as he grinned at his mother. "What about Aunt Ellie's money? Can't I use that, just until payday on Monday?"

"Who said I had any of Ellie's money?"

"I was listening. I know she won't be back for the $500 until next Friday." Troy patted his mother's arm. "How about it? I can get those skis on sale today, have the weekend at Snow Valley, and pay you back on Monday."

Madge felt uneasy about the deal although she wanted to encourage her son. Troy had made some new friends who were skiers. He seemed to be leaving the "bad apples" behind, along with his old drug habit. He's just "borrowing" the money for a few days, she thought. "OK, Troy, go ahead."

But Monday brought unexpected problems. Troy broke his leg on the slopes. He had hospital and doctor bills to pay, and no health insurance. Troy needed his paycheck for his release from the hospital.

With Ellie's money all gone, Madge was ashamed to face her sister. She saw herself as dishonest and untrustworthy. She had stolen money that Ellie needed to rent an apartment. It was the same as if she had taken it out of her sister's purse without any regard for Ellie's plans.

How could she make this up to her? And what kind of lesson was this for Troy, adding to his immediate problems with cast and crutches?

But mother and son were accomplices in the mess. Why hadn't she thought this through so she could be a role model for her son and keep her own self-esteem intact?

She picked up the want ads for the third time but could not concentrate on her job search. Madge felt worthless. Why would anyone want to hire her?

You can't live your best life, wrote M. Scott Peck, when you're telling lies. When you're dishonest, you don't like yourself much, as Madge discovered. That's a strong reason to be honest.

Look at your family, neighborhood, nation, and universe. God's love enfolds both your neighbors and yourself. You don't want to harm yourself or your neighbors with dishonest actions. Integrity helps everyone and points the way to God and enables others to see him.

Making a Difference

Patrick Reynolds, grandson of the founder of America's largest tobacco company, is trying to turn the family reputation around by honestly helping others. About 10 years ago Patrick sold off his stock in R. J. Reynolds Industries, Inc., believing that cigarettes have "killed many millions of people." He said the source of his family wealth is poison, and he feels responsible to tell people the truth.

Because of his nonsmoking activism, he has put himself in an awkward position with his relatives. Patrick's brothers, all heavy smokers and stockholders in the Reynolds empire, wonder why anyone with the "most famous name in tobacco would bite the hand that fed him."

"I saw I could make a difference and do something with my life," said the 40-year-old crusader whose memories include a chain-smoking father, always out of breath, who died of emphysema at age 58, "and find my place in the universe."

Reynolds discovered that not everyone agreed with his standards of honesty. Your family and friends may look at things another way, too. In the many communities of our world, there are different codes of what's acceptable. Standards vary from neighborhood to neighborhood, state to state, nation to nation. What goes and what doesn't is largely determined by ordinary citizens. And that's a good reason for holding firmly to the principles of honesty that our Christian faith teaches us.

Looking up at Heroes

We all have a role in setting community values, and so do our public heroes. The world cheered when Canadian Ben Johnson won his medals. But when lab tests snitched on his use of muscle-enhancing steroids, his fans were shocked. All the medals were stripped from the disgraced Olympian.

In a sports scandal such as this, community values are the ultimate losers, said columnist George Will. The public's standards become corrupted, too. For example, use of steroids among high school boys has already reached epidemic proportions.

Look at the popularity of sports events and the huge amount of money involved. We invest our time and emotions as we enshrine our sports heroes. We don't want to believe that our heroes can topple.

"Sports is valued," Will wrote in the *Los Angeles Times*, "because it builds character." But too many athletes don't understand why rules prohibit chemical additives. The players themselves haven't considered the value of winning.

Doesn't winning mean that the one player is better than other competitors performing under the same circumstances? If that's true, then unfair competition is pointless. Use of dangerous chemicals by some competitors is unfair.

Fairness and honesty are community principles that we must encourage everywhere—in sports, government, business, and education. Crumbling standards in those areas will erode our family values.

More than students are hurt in school scandals, says Stanford education professor Nel Noddings. In a November 8, 1988, article in the *Los Angeles Times*, Sam Enriquez quoted Noddings: "Cheating shatters the foundation of the community. It's not just a matter of breaking the rules. Kids need to learn that professional and community life depend on the trust we put in each other."

Almost all cultures and traditions recommend fairness, honesty, and accountability, said Michael Josephson, founder of the Institute for the Advancement of Ethics, in a TV appearance on "Bill Moyer's World of Ideas." That doesn't mean these values are practiced by everyone, but at least the ideal is there. Almost everyone recognizes the fundamentals for honest behavior.

Basically, caring about other people keeps us from cheating them. Except in unusual circumstances, we don't lie to someone we love. One basic reason for being honest is neighborly love.

In our attempts to treat others fairly, we set our values. By striving to be honest we define priorities. By aiming for honesty and fairness we articulate our goals.

Taking a Stand

Sometimes when acting out of honesty the situation takes a wild turn. We feel we must do what is right for the community—we can't live with ourselves if we don't—but end up getting sand kicked in our eyes.

Robyn worked in the investment department of a large firm. She dealt with printers and typesetters who produced company mailings sent to potential investors. She liked her job until she found out what her boss was doing, and a lawyer gave her unsettling advice.

A returned letter, postage due, was the tip-off that Robyn's boss, Elsbeth, was soliciting her own list of investors with insider information. The clerk in the mailroom shared the misdirected letter with Robyn.

"It's illegal, you know," the mail clerk told Robyn. "She's using the company letterhead. That's why I opened it."

"This could be big trouble," agreed Robyn. "The securities commission might find out."

Next, the printer who did most of their work phoned Robyn. He said Elsbeth was threatening to find another printer if he didn't invest in her "special offering." That's illegal coercion, Robyn thought.

She assured the printer that he would continue to receive their company's sizable printing order. Privately, she anguished over what she should do if Elsbeth told her otherwise.

If Robyn confronted her boss about the insider trading, she would be making a serious accusation. Elsbeth might fire her or retaliate in some other way.

That week Robyn's husband was meeting with a lawyer friend about a small business deal they were working on. Robyn had a chance to ask the lawyer for advice.

"If you don't blow the whistle on your boss before she's caught," warned the lawyer, "you'll be in big trouble, too."

"Why me? I haven't done anything wrong."

"In the eyes of the law you have," the lawyer said. "Both the mail clerk and the printer told you what your boss is doing and you didn't do anything about it."

Robyn couldn't sleep that night. By morning she knew she had to talk to the company president.

The president took action. After several months of turmoil, Elsbeth was transferred to another division and Robyn was fired. She had trouble getting another job right away because her record appeared to be tainted. Robyn found it difficult to convince potential employers that she had done nothing wrong.

What kind of a reward is that? Is this supposed to be an argument for acting honestly?

We have no promises of gold stars for every good deed. Some of our acts of mercy may be ignored by our peers, but our reason for doing such deeds is not for their applause. In fact, we may bring hardships upon ourselves by doing the right thing. Our integrity may motivate us to do something for a higher good that in some way will hurt our family. But God calls us to live by higher standards than the world around us.

We must look at the ripple effect of Robyn's actions to see the good reasons to be honest. Just as throwing a pebble into a pond sends circles throughout the water, Robyn's honest whistle-blowing reached out beyond her personal life to a larger community.

For one thing, her family was proud of her and supported her actions. The printer admired her integrity and helped her find work. Robyn's actions had a profound impact on other coworkers' values. She had done a service for the investment community, and Robyn thinks that's a good reason to do the right thing.

The results of acting out your principles by speaking up and doing the honest thing may make a huge difference in bettering other people's lives. Modern Chinese writer Liu Binyan told about a worker's action against a corrupt leader, Comrade Wang Shouxin.

This ruthless woman had amassed a fortune from her many dishonest deals. Wang had a loyal following who profited from her frauds and sang her praises. The only ones remaining silent were the abused workers.

Liu wrote in *People or Monsters?* that they were "humble, careful, diligent, conscientious, hard working and plain living" people afraid to step forward. As a result,

Comrade Wang became more arrogant as her gang victimized even more of the meek workers.

"Reward and punishment were turned upside down. Truth yielded to falsity. The goodhearted were ruled by the vicious." Liu quoted an old Chinese saying: "Everything is messed up by people who are afraid of offending others."

One worker stood out, saying he "would not close his eyes when he died" if he did not topple the corrupt brigade leader first.

Liu's true story of this one man's successful efforts against dishonesty and graft brought a remarkable response from Chinese readers in the late 1980s. Workers became willing to stand up for honesty to improve their work unit, community, and country. The ripple caused by the worker immortalized in Liu's book may eventually affect a large percentage of China's one billion people.

In fact, the courageous uprisings of the Chinese students in the summer of 1989 may be just such an example. Many of the young people who stood on their convictions lost their lives, but the world will not forget.

Honesty is more than a beacon of God's truth. Honesty and integrity are the very essence of our community life together—whether that community consists of dozens or hundreds or millions of people.

We will find that striving to be honest helps us to be able to get up in the morning with courage, stand a little straighter and walk with pride. What we need is more practice.

Questions for Reflection or Discussion

1. What are your primary reasons for being honest? List three or four.

2. If sometimes you fall short of your own standards (are dishonest, tell a lie, withhold information on your taxes), what do you do? How do you make amends? How does God's love for you fit into the picture?

3. Often our heroes have feet of clay. Have you ever discovered some lack of integrity in people you greatly admired? How did you feel?

4. Think of people from history or our own day who dared to take a stand on an unpopular issue. What gave them the courage to do what they did?

7

How Can I Grow in Honesty?

Then we will no longer be infants, tossed back and forth
by the waves, and blown here and there
by every wind . . .

—Ephesians 4:14

A Georgian lawyer, Bobby Lee Cook, had a reputation for forcing witnesses to focus on the unvarnished truth. In the *Los Angeles Times* on July 30, 1986, he said he had "a country feelin' if somethin' ain't right."

When he suspected that a state's witness was making things up, Cook used the weather to help the young man grow in honesty. Storm clouds were gathering in the summer sky.

"Now, you know that's a lie, and you're not telling the truth," Cook said. "You're lying, aren't you?"

The open courthouse windows revealed the sultry reality of thunderheads. The witness answered, "No, sir."

Ominous rumbles interrupted the questioning. A bolt of lightning flashed across the faces of those facing the window; a thunderclap startled the bailiff. Cook only increased the intensity of his gaze on the witness, who was leaning forward, hanging onto the arms of his chair. Cook slowly pointed one finger toward heaven.

"Oh," the young man confessed. "I've been lying, Mr. Bobby Lee. I've been lying."

To grow in honesty, you don't actually need a thunderclap, a bolt of lightning, or a prosecuting attorney to point out the way to start. Instead of lightning, you can look to the light of the world.

You are a branch of the vine that is Christ. You can listen to God's Spirit within you and act with loving concern toward your neighbor, as toward yourself.

The next step toward a more honest life is to face the reality of the world where you live. There are temptations to be dishonest everywhere, in your inner struggles, personal relationships, family, and community life. Do you always see them?

Stumbling Blocks

You need to identify the pitfalls, even if it's just rearranging cards in a harmless game of solitaire. Maybe it's your diet or the aerobics class.

In the same way that New Year's Day is a wonderful 24-hour period for keeping new resolutions, you can start every day of the year with a clean slate. God has forgiven the misdealing of aces and kings in solitaire and the bending of your knees so you could touch your toes in aerobics class.

Accept the free forgiveness God offers us through Christ and start anew. It naturally follows that you can also grant forgiveness to those who have hurt you. They, too, are starting over.

After facing reality, consider the long-view of your actions. You can see that dishonesty hurts yourself, your family, and your community. You see honesty as a better way to grow, with forgiveness as the key.

That's when you start looking at your values, at Christian principles such as justice, responsibility, and concern for others. Check the values of your everyday life. Examine the qualities you admire in people and in policies that govern your life. Decide what makes something worthwhile.

What does a diploma mean, for example, if the school's teachers are manipulating rating scores and grades? Every position of expertise is now suspect. The daily news keeps you informed about the latest in corruption and fraud. If you don't like the dishonesty you see around you, can you reach out to make a difference in your community?

Cocoonery

People today stay in their cocoons too long, says a research professor from the University of Florida in Gainesville. Dr. Marvin Harris has studied social changes in Americans since World War II. He says some people have retreated into mysticism or cults to avoid the harsh reality of a dishonest world.

The sociologist reported in a speech in May 1988 at California State University, Northridge, that modern folks no longer take a hard look at their own lives. They not only don't look at themselves, they don't look around much at others, either. Most citizens have no sense of community responsibility and do not vote.

For a better world, you need to consider the big picture. That includes your neighbors.

Driving faster than the speed limit may be an individual's approach to a bureaucratic regulation. Installing a radar detector in your car seems to be a way to outsmart that ticket-happy cop hiding behind the billboard. But there is more to it than that. To grow in honesty you need to see your daily life from several perspectives different from your own.

That means taking off your blinders and coming out of your cocoon. You need to help your family and neighbors come out and grow, too.

A suburban community near San Francisco has started talking about values. School administrators, teachers, and parents in San Ramon say they will go beyond academic concerns to address the question of "how to raise good kids."

"Everyone wants his child to grow up to be helpful and responsible; to be a good citizen," says San Ramon Valley Superintendent William Streshly. "No one wants to see his child become an immoral, scheming, rich drug dealer. Even gangsters want their children to be moral."

Reaching Out

Programs like that one demonstrate ways to cope with dishonesty, cheating, and other moral concerns. As Joan Libman noted in her *Los Angeles Times* article, the idea is catching hold in other communities. A Maryland school administrator, Mary Ellen Sterlie, said their program cancels out standards kids learn from TV, rock music, and their peers' values.

Los Angeles third graders in a special program are learning environmental responsibility for their actions. The Law in a Free Society Project, based in Calabasas, California, explains to elementary students justice, responsibility, freedom, and participation in their community. Such curricula changes can mark a beginning toward overcoming dishonesty.

Parents say results from these programs have been remarkable. Children in one class showed more sensitivity, for example, after a talk by a child in a wheelchair. She explained what it felt like to be teased. In another school, a buddy system for tutoring matched advanced students with younger ones. It paid off with less friction in the playground. Bullies became big brothers.

How do sensitivity and concern for others affect your struggles with dishonesty? When you are sensitive to others' feelings, you don't want to hurt them or take advantage of them.

In a 1988 TV appearance on "Bill Moyers' World of Ideas," Sissela Bok, author and philosopher, said we should practice honesty in our own lives "politically and publicly, to begin to turn the tide." She talked of "rolling back the amount of violence, the amount of lying, the amount of breaches of promise and of law."

Practicing Honesty

By practicing honesty in our lives, can we affect decisions made by huge corporations? Did public apathy toward honesty influence that Ford executive who chose to ignore the Pinto's faulty gasoline tank? Public opinion may be slow to gather force, but when it finally erupts it is extremely powerful.

When a large brokerage firm recently committed security fraud involving $650 million, did you realize there was a connection with your own life? James Flanagan, writing in the *Los Angeles Times*, said that caper meant lost jobs for millions of people. The various businesses involved are the "lifeblood of your communities." As a consumer, you are the real victim of corporate fraud.

"Few people are so naive," Flanagan wrote in his December 22, 1988, article, "that they confuse Wall Street with Sunday school." But they fail to see big business as their concern. Instead, they shrug their shoulders, thinking that's the way the corporate world works.

We need to face the reality of living in a dishonest world, to be sensitive to others, and to see our own missteps. Sissela Bok says that when we practice deceit in order to win and benefit ourselves, we must stop and consider our opponents. "How would I feel if I were on that other side?" she says. "Well, next time I may be on the other side. In fact, these very same people who say they're my friends now may need, for their particular purposes, to lie to me tomorrow." The Golden Rule is a good guide to follow. If we want others to treat us fairly, then we need to practice fairness with them, too.

To grow in honesty we must ask other questions, too. What kind of mindset of misguided loyalty occurs in gangs, ethnic groups, political parties, social clubs, schools, and even some families? Is it blind partisanship when we follow along in dishonesty without question?

Pathological loyalty is what Bok calls a partisanship that has gone too far. "We say we can do anything to those other people—we can send terrorists into their country, we can spew forth disinformation, we can do anything."

Bok says it's up to individuals to ensure that the government doesn't slip. We need to remind ourselves constantly that every dishonest decision—individual, governmental, and corporate—affects everyone.

To ignore that reality is cocoonery, and we need to break free. In *People of the Lie*, author M. Scott Peck says such isolation is partly the result of specialization. We focus only on our own particular job, hobby, single-subject magazine, radio stations that play "our" kind of music, and other specialized media. Communication analysts say "*narrow* casting" has supplanted *broad*casting.

Connecting Members

To practice honesty we need to be reminded of the connecting links between members of our diverse population. We must recognize the sisterhood and brotherhood we share with others.

Struggling through daily decisions, we are prodded by as many as 3,000 advertising messages. Billboards, radio and TV commercials, sky writing, tags on our clothing, and imprints on pens and glassware bombard us daily. Some advertising is dishonest, such as aiming tobacco and alcohol ads at children.

Did you know that market researchers simply refer to you as a "head"? Advertisers want as many heads as possible watching their commercials so they can turn your "wants" into "needs." You become a part of the great shopping mall society, whether you like it or not.

These advertising dispatches need to be supplemented by jolting queries to keep you practicing honesty in every situation. The following questions, derived from previous examples dealing with problems of deceit, can be guidelines for growth:

- Who will benefit from my actions?
- Will anyone be hurt?
- Will my actions bring good?
- Will my actions bring evil?
- What is the greater good?
- What is the lesser evil?
- What will be the end result?
- Am I acting out of loving concern?
- Why do I want to be honest?
- How do I stay honest?

The questions aren't easy. You may not be able to come up with answers for all of them. Just when you think you know what the end results of your actions will be, you may think of another consequence, and another, and another.

Don't give up. Keep probing. There will be situations when you won't stop to ask these questions. You will operate on automatic pilot, only to consider your actions later, or maybe not at all. The questions are meant to make you aware of various possibilities of honesty or dishonesty in difficult decisions. They are not meant to make you immobile with doubts.

The hardest questions are the last two: why and how should we be honest? Answering these important questions is a key to your personal creed. You may find your motivation in earlier questions, such as who will benefit, or will it bring good.

You can ask yourself how God intends you to live. Remind yourself that serving your neighbor is serving God. Keep reading the Bible, pray regularly, participate in your church's worship services and classes, read books and newspapers, and keep thinking and exploring.

Don't worry about mistakes. We are not perfect, but are like the clay pots Paul wrote about in 2 Corinthians. We are full of imperfections and flaws that are important parts of our creation, and give us strength. "We are often troubled, but not crushed; sometimes in doubt, but never in despair; there are many enemies, but we are never without a friend; and though badly hurt at times, we are not destroyed" (2 Cor. 4:8-9 Today's English Version).

There is hope that we can survive in a dishonest world and, more than that, we can be proud of ourselves for our efforts. With practice, we grow in honesty. With loving concern, we help our family and our neighbors. We serve God. We may be clay pots but we shine with reflected light.

Questions for Reflection or Discussion

1. Have you or people you know been tempted to withdraw from the realities of this dishonest world (stay in a cocoon)? What happens to the problems of society when too many people make this choice?

2. How can we "raise good kids"? Do you know of examples similar to the ones the author describes in the section "Reaching Out"?

3. Review the 10 questions on page 89. Choose an action that has some controversial elements and go through the 10 questions. (Example: I picket a company because they're doing something dishonest or wrong.)

Afterword

Christian Integrity Checklist

Expanding on the commandment from Matthew 22:37-39, loving God, neighbor, and self, I offer the following suggestions to help you maintain your integrity in a dishonest world.

God

Celebrate the fact that God created you.
Accept God's love and forgiveness through Christ.
Let God's Spirit guide your conscience and your actions.
Read the Bible and apply it to your life.
Pray, both listening to God and talking with God.
Know that God's Spirit lives within you.
Confess your misdeeds, make amends, and accept forgiveness.

Neighbor

Love, accept, and forgive your neighbors.
Be a responsible role model.
See individuals instead of faceless groups.
Be open to others' viewpoints, even if different from yours.
Listen to your neighbors.
Empathize with other people's feelings.
Consider consequences when you take action or fail to act.
Look for unstated contracts with others.
Allow your neighbor the same freedom you enjoy.

Self

Love, accept, and forgive yourself.
Affirm that life is precious.
Share yourself with others.
Think, ponder, and examine your values.
Become informed on issues related to honesty and dishonesty.
Let yourself be guided by Scripture and prayer.
Keep remembering how much God loves you.

Bibliography

Adams, Robert. *Badmouth*. Berkeley: University of California Press, 1977.

Baker, Roland. *Liars' Manual*. Chicago: Nelson-Hall, 1983.

Bok, Sissela. *Lying: Moral Choice in Public and Private Life*. New York: Random House, 1979.

————. *Secrets: On the Ethics of Concealment and Revelation*. New York: Pantheon, 1983.

————. "Bill Moyer's World of Ideas," TV show #116, Oct. 3, 1988.

Bowyer, J. Barton. *Cheating*. New York: St. Martin's Press, 1982.

Conn, Walter. *Conscience: Development and Self-Transcendence*. Birmingham, AL: Religious Education Press, 1980.

Eck, Marcel. *Lies and Truth*. New York: Macmillan, 1970.

Ekman, Paul. *Telling Lies*. New York: Berkley Publishing, 1986.

Griffiths, R. *A Study of Imagination in Early Childhood*. London: Kegan Paul, Trench, Trubner, 1945.

Hall, G. Stanley. "Children's Lies." *American Journal of Psychology*. Jan. 1980, Vol. 3, pp 59-70.

Healy, William and Mary Tenney. *Pathological Lying, Accusation, and Swindling*. Montclair, NJ: Patterson Smith, 1915.

Hiers, Richard H. *Jesus and Ethics.* Philadelphia: Westminster Press, 1968.

Keillor, Garrison. *Lake Wobegon Days.* New York: Viking, 1985.

Knight, James. *Conscience and Guilt.* New York: Appleton-Century-Crofts, 1969.

Levinas, Emmanuel. *Ethics and Infinity.* Pittsburgh: Duquesne, 1985.

Liu, Binyan. *People or Monstors?* Bloomington, IN: Indiana University Press, 1983.

Ludwig, Arnold. *Importance of Lying.* Springfield, IL: C. C. Thomas, 1965.

Maddox, Donald. *Semiotics of Deceit.* Cranberry, NJ: Bucknell University Press, 1984.

Maguire, Daniel C. *The Moral Choice.* Garden City, NY: Doubleday, 1978.

Mars, Gerald. *Cheats at Work.* London: George Allen & Umvin, 1982.

Martin, Mike and Roland Schinzinger. *Ethics in Engineering.* New York: McGraw Hill, 1988.

Martin, Robert. *The Paradox of the Liar.* Atascadero, CA: Ridgeview, 1979.

Milton, John. "Aeropagitica." An index to the Columbia edition of John Milton. New York: Columbia University Press, 1940.

Pearson, W. "Character and Education of Our Youth." *Vital Speeches of the Day*, April 15, 1986.

Peck, M. Scott. *People of the Lie.* New York: Simon & Schuster, 1985.

Piper, John. *Love Your Enemies.* Cambridge: Cambridge University Press, 1980.

Priestley, J. B. *Angel Pavement.* Chicago: University of Chicago Press, 1958.

Rattigan, Terence. *The Winslow Boy.* New York: Grove, 1982.

Schneider, Jennifer. *Back from Betrayal.* New York: Harper & Row, 1988.

Wells, H. G. "A Slip under the Microscope." *Complete Short Stories of H. G. Wells.* London: Benn, 1966.

———. *Tono-Bungay.* Lincoln, NE: University of Nebraska Press, 1978.

Westermarck, Edward. *Christianity and Morals.* Salem, NH: Ayer Company, 1939.